GRIZZLY
DAD

FOR LOUISE AND HER DAD

Joanna Harrison

David Fickling Books

Dad woke up in a

GRRRRIZZLY mood!

All morning he grrroaned

and grrrizzled . . .

and GRRRUMPED!

And then he went back to bed . . .

He was just like a bear with a sore head.

When Mum had finished clearing up, she and my little brother and sister had to go out.

"Go and see how Dad is," she said as they left, so I went upstairs to wake him up.

"Dad," I whispered, but he only grunted.

"Dad!" I said, but he only snuffled.

"DAD!!!" I yelled, and pulled back the bedcovers.

But it wasn't Dad
in bed at all . . .

It was a GREAT BIG

GRIZZLY BEAR!

I should have been frightened,
but the grumpy look on its face
reminded me of someone.

"Dad," I said. "Is that you?"

The bear rushed off to look
in the bathroom mirror.
He grunted miserably.

"Don't worry, Dad," I said.
"I'll look after you!"

So I wiped
his eyes,

combed
his hair,

brushed
his teeth

(he was a bit SMELLY)

and gave him breakfast. BUT now that Dad was a
bear, his manners were really quite AWFUL!

And when he started rummaging around
in the fridge, I'd had enough.

"DAD!" I said.
"I'm FED UP with you!!
First you're in a BAD mood,
then you turn into a BEAR!
And now
you're making
a horrible
MESS!!!"

Dad looked at me
in a funny sort of way,
and before I knew it . . .

. . . we were off, heading into town.

VRRROOM!!!

First we went to the cinema.
We had the whole place to ourselves!

I was beginning to realize that having a grizzly bear as a dad wasn't so bad after all.

Then we went to the park. I taught Dad how to skateboard,

and he taught me how to scratch my back and climb trees.

And how to just lie about . . .

doing nothing at all.

When we got home, we made honey sandwiches and watched soccer on the television.

It had been the best day EVER.

"Thanks, Dad," I said. "You're the GREATEST, even if you are a bear!"

Then Dad did what dads do best—he gave me

a GREAT BIG

BEAR HUG!!

And when I looked up,
he wasn't a bear anymore.

Suddenly, Mum came back and everything
returned to normal.

WELL . . . ALMOST . . .

"What a MESS!" said Mum.
"This place looks just like a pigsty!"

"Sorry," we grunted,
and trotted off
to clear it up.

A DAVID FICKLING BOOK

Published by David Fickling Books
an imprint of Random House Children's Books
a division of Random House, Inc.
New York

Copyright © 2008 by Joanna Harrison

Visit us on the Web! www.randomhouse.com/kids

Educators and librarians, for a variety of teaching tools, visit us at www.randomhouse.com/teachers

Library of Congress Cataloging-in-Publication Data is available on request.

ISBN: 978-0-385-75173-5(trade) — ISBN: 978-0-385-75174-2(lib. bdg)

MANUFACTURED IN CHINA

10 9 8 7 6 5 4 3 2 1

May 2009

First American Edition